DAVID

Plays Hide-and-Seek in Folktales

Juega al Escondite en Cuentos Folklóricos

by Dolores Mayorga

Translated from the Spanish
by Lori Ann Schatschneider

Lerner Publications Company • Minneapolis

This edition published 1992
by Lerner Publications Company
241 First Avenue North
Minneapolis, Minnesota 55401 USA

Originally published as *David juega al escondite en los cuentos*
by Editorial Planeta, S.A., Barcelona, Spain
© Dolores Mayorga, 1989

Translation copyright © 1992 by Lerner Publications Company
Translated from the Spanish by Lori Ann Schatschneider

Library of Congress Cataloging-in-Publication Data

Mayorga, Dolores.
    [David juega al escondite en los cuentos. English &
Spanish]
    David plays hide-and-seek in folktales = David juega al
escondite en cuentos folklóricos / by Dolores Mayorga ;
translated from the Spanish by Lori Ann Schatschneider.
        p.   cm.
    Translation of: David juega al escondite en los cuentos.
    Summary: The reader may search for David and his
friends in the lands of folktales.
    ISBN 0-8225-2003-6
    [1. Characters and characteristics in literature—Fiction.
2. Picture puzzles. 3. Spanish language materials—
Bilingual.] I. Title. II. Title: David juega al escondite en
cuentos folklóricos.
PZ73.M35   1992
[Fic]—dc20   91-48046
                                               CIP
                                               AC

Manufactured in the United States of America

1 2 3 4 5 6 7 8 9 10 01 00 99 98 97 96 95 94 93 92

David plays hide-and-seek through the
lands of folktales. He visits towns, forests,
deserts, and castles. Paula, on her bicycle,
and Little Bear also try to pass by unnoticed.

*David juega al escondite a través de las
tierras de los cuentos folklóricos. Visita
pueblos, bosques, desiertos, y castillos. Paula,
en su bicicleta, y Osito procuran pasar
inadvertidos también.*

Who will wake
Sleeping Beauty?

¿Quién despertará
a la Bella Durmiente?

•••••••••••••••••••••••••••••

David, Paula, and Little Bear
are hiding. Can you find them
and these other things too?

*David, Paula, y Osito se esconden.
¿Puedes encontrar a ellos y estas
otras cosas también?*

•••••••••••••••••••••••••••••

chess game
ajedrez

unicorn
unicornio

fairies
hadas

donkey
burro

spinning wheel
torno de hilar

court jesters
bufones

blue cape
capa azul

king and queen
rey y reina

fire
fuego

David is in the desert with Ali Baba and the forty thieves.

David está en el desierto con Alí Babá y los cuarenta ladrones.

••••••••••••••••••••••••••••••

David, Paula, and Little Bear are hiding. Can you find them and these other things too?

David, Paula, y Osito se esconden. ¿Puedes encontrar a ellos y estas otras cosas también?

••••••••••••••••••••••••••••••

snake charmer
encantador de serpientes

cave
cueva

ten jugs
diez cántaros

salamander
salamandra

white sail
vela blanca

treasure
tesoro

baby
bebé

chicks
pollitos

potatoes
patatas

What is Puss in Boots doing?

¿Qué hace el Gato con Botas?

••••••••••••••••••••••••••••••

David, Paula, and Little Bear are hiding. Can you find them and these other things too?

David, Paula, y Osito se esconden. ¿Puedes encontrar a ellos y estas otras cosas también?

••••••••••••••••••••••••••••••

archers
arqueros

melons
melones

wild boar
jabalí

duel
torneo

seven castles
siete castillos

crown
corona

swimmer
nadador

two red feathers
dos plumas rojas

seeds
semillas

What will happen when Jack plants the magic beans?

¿Qué va a ocurrir cuando Jack siembra las habas mágicas?

• •

David, Paula, and Little Bear are hiding. Can you find them and these other things too?

David, Paula, y Osito se esconden. ¿Puedes encontrar a ellos y estas otras cosas también?

• •

jewelry
joyería

hay
heno

barrels
barriles

nine trees
nueve árboles

fabric
telas

sacks of flour
sacos de harina

cauliflowers
coliflores

rug
alfombra

giant
gigante

David follows the Pied Piper of Hamelin.

David sigue al flautista de Hamelín.

◆◆◆◆◆◆◆◆◆◆◆◆◆◆◆◆◆◆◆◆◆◆◆◆◆◆◆◆◆◆

David, Paula, and Little Bear are hiding. Can you find them and these other things too?

David, Paula, y Osito se esconden. ¿Puedes encontrar a ellos y estas otras cosas también?

◆◆◆◆◆◆◆◆◆◆◆◆◆◆◆◆◆◆◆◆◆◆◆◆◆◆◆◆◆◆

well
pozo

slingshot
tirachinas

wheelbarrow
carretilla

music
música

hammer
martillo

rats
ratas

arrows
flechas

ladder
escalera

toy car
cochecito

Cinderella and the Prince dance, but only until midnight.

Cenicienta y el Príncipe bailan, pero sólo hasta la medianoche.

••••••••••••••••••••••••••

David, Paula, and Little Bear are hiding. Can you find them and these other things too?

David, Paula, y Osito se esconden. ¿Puedes encontrar a ellos y estas otras cosas también?

••••••••••••••••••••••••••

five waiters
cinco camareros

mask
máscara

carriage
carruaje

fish
pescado

three violins
tres violines

water pitcher
jarro de agua

turkey
pavo

two swords
dos espadas

pink purse
bolso rosado

Who's afraid of the Big Bad Wolf?

¿Quién le tiene miedo al Lobo Feroz?

••••••••••••••••••••••••••••••

David, Paula, and Little Bear are hiding. Can you find them and these other things too?

David, Paula, y Osito se esconden. ¿Puedes encontrar a ellos y estas otras cosas también?

••••••••••••••••••••••••••••••

Three Little Pigs
los Tres Cerditos

lambs
corderos

Little Red Riding Hood
Caperucita Roja

grandmother
abuelita

scarecrow
espantapájaros

raccoons
mapaches

binoculars
binóculos

hammock
hamaca

rocking chair
mecedora

David goes to the forest with Snow White and Hansel and Gretel.

Se va David al bosque con Blancanieves y Hansel y Gretel.

◆◆◆◆◆◆◆◆◆◆◆◆◆◆◆◆◆◆◆◆◆

David, Paula, and Little Bear are hiding. Can you find them and these other things too?

David, Paula, y Osito se esconden. ¿Puedes encontrar a ellos y estas otras cosas también?

◆◆◆◆◆◆◆◆◆◆◆◆◆◆◆◆◆◆◆◆◆

Seven Dwarves
Siete Enanitos

axe
hacha

firefighters
bomberos

canoe
canoa

two runners
dos corredores

coal
carbón

knapsacks
mochilas

yellow candies
caramelos amarillos

owl
búho

Aladdin has a
magic lamp.

*Aladino tiene una
lámpara mágica.*

•••••••••••••••••••••••••••••••

David, Paula, and Little Bear
are hiding. Can you find them
and these other things too?

*David, Paula, y Osito se esconden.
¿Puedes encontrar a ellos y estas
otras cosas también?*

•••••••••••••••••••••••••••••••

swan
cisne

five kites
cinco cometas

genie
genio

two fans
dos abanicos

mountains
montañas

chopsticks
palillos

black beard
barba negra

snow
nieve

bridge
puente

David helps the people of Lilliput tie down the giant!

¡David ayuda a la gente de Lilliput en atar el gigante!

....

David, Paula, and Little Bear are hiding. Can you find them and these other things too?

David, Paula, y Osito se esconden. ¿Puedes encontrar a ellos y estas otras cosas también?

....

hang glider
deslizador

cannon
cañón

golf clubs
palos de golf

barber
peluquero

button
botón

three guards
tres guardias

ice cream vendor
vendedor de helados

city wall
muro

buckles
hebillas

About the Author and Illustrator
Dolores Mayorga lives in Barcelona, Spain, with
her husband and three children, where she writes and
illustrates children's books. Her favorite folktale is *Cinderella*.
A romantic at heart, she is enchanted by fairies,
princes, and happy endings.

Sobre la Autora y Artisa
*Dolores Mayorga vive en Barcelona, España, con su esposo
y sus tres hijos, donde escribe y ilustra libros para niños.
Su cuento favorito es* Cinderella. *Una romántica en el fondo,
le encantan hadas, príncipes, y conclusiones alegres.*